W9-ALV-511

DISCARD

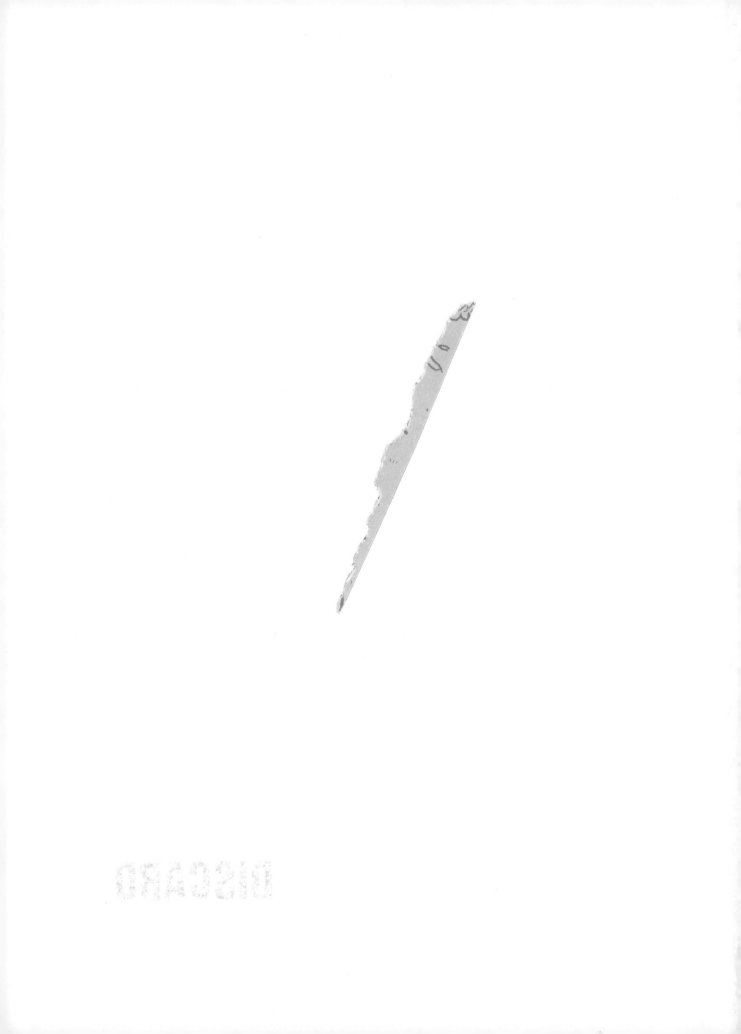

DISCARD

LEAP!

For JoJo, our magical mover and shaker, who keeps us
(Daddy, Mommy, Sophie and Ashey) leaping! — J.A.B.L.

For Margot. May your life be always an adventure. — J.B.

Text © 2017 JonArno Lawson
Illustrations © 2017 Josée Bisaillon

All rights reserved. No part of this publication may be reproduced,
stored in a retrieval system or transmitted, in any form or by any means, without
the prior written permission of Kids Can Press Ltd. or, in case of photocopying or
other reprographic copying, a license from The Canadian Copyright Licensing
Agency (Access Copyright). For an Access Copyright license, visit
www.accesscopyright.ca or call toll free to 1-800-893-5777.

Kids Can Press gratefully acknowledges the financial support of
the Government of Ontario, through the Ontario Media Development Corporation,
the Ontario Arts Council, the Canada Council for the Arts and the Government
of Canada, through the CBF, for our publishing activity.

Published in Canada and the U.S. by Kids Can Press Ltd.
25 Dockside Drive, Toronto, ON M5A 0B5

Kids Can Press is a Corus Entertainment Inc. company
www.kidscanpress.com

The artwork in this book was rendered in mixed media.
The text is set in Clue.

Edited by Yvette Ghione
Designed by Julia Naimska

Printed and bound in Shenzhen, China, in 3/2017 by C&C Offset

CM 17 0 9 8 7 6 5 4 3 2 1

Library and Archives Canada Cataloguing in Publication

Lawson, JonArno, author
Leap! / written by JonArno Lawson ; illustrated by Josée Bisaillon.

ISBN 978-1-77138-678-4 (hardback)

I. Bisaillon, Josée, 1982–, illustrator II. Title.

PS8573.A93L43 2017   jC813'.54   C2016-906543-X

LEAP!

JonArno Lawson

Illustrated by

Josée Bisaillon

Kids Can Press

A flea asleep
in the deep green moss
nettled by midges
wakes up cross —
he starts to fidget
and turn and toss.
Lever-legs twitch to

LEAP!

into the path
of a little grasshopper
and that sets her jumping —
no one can stop her —

glide, land,
leap and glide —
tilting a little from side to side
down and up to

LEAP!

And away ...

onto a bunny
down where the flowers
and the grass smell sunny.

Bug on her head?
Suddenly haunches
tauten tight to

LEAP!

Land!
Twist and spin!
The bunny bounds out
as the clouds roll in.
A dog gets a whiff
and barks at the wind —
bouncing, bouncing, springing
  and lunging!
Down the bank that dog goes
  plunging.
Gambol, lurch to

LEAP!

Crash
into the lake,
scaring the lake fish
wide awake.
They break the surface with a
flip, flop, shake!

Tails go smack!
Silvery skins —
slippery slap!
Flashing fins —

under again then
back to the top to

LEAP!

and splash
right back down
to knock off a bullfrog's
lily-pad crown.
The pond prince shows
his inflatable frown —

trudgening lightly,
croaking and nervous,
over the top of the
rippling surface —

webbed feet flatten,
cheeks re-fatten,
legs stretch long to

LEAP!

high
onto the bank
(he scrambled up
then down he sank)
next to the nose
of a high-strung horse,
standing to drink
after running her course.

The horse, astounded,
can't make sense
of the frog
and draws back, eyes immense,
rearing tall to

LEAP!

straight up and
over the fence,
where the dog sits crouching,
ready and tense ...

Happy barks
meet startled snorts
as she goes leaping after
the leaping horse.

West, east,
south and north,
around in circles
back
and forth

on all fours finally,
bowing low to

LEAP!

But she can't keep up.
The deep green moss
is a little too deep
and a little too soft ...

There are too many ridges
and bridges to cross.

She stops to pant
and chew at a burr —
the flea sees his chance
and leaps on her.

They both lie down
and turn and toss,
then hunker down to

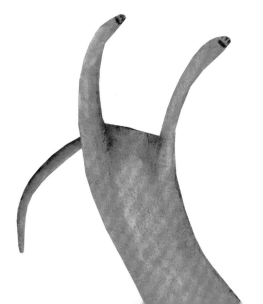

sleep.

JAN   2018